DELPHINE DURAND   translated by

my house

MY HOUSE DOESN'T LOOK ANYTHING SPECIAL

MY HOUSE ISN'T FANCY ON THE OUTSIDE

Really, nothing special at all

COME IN →

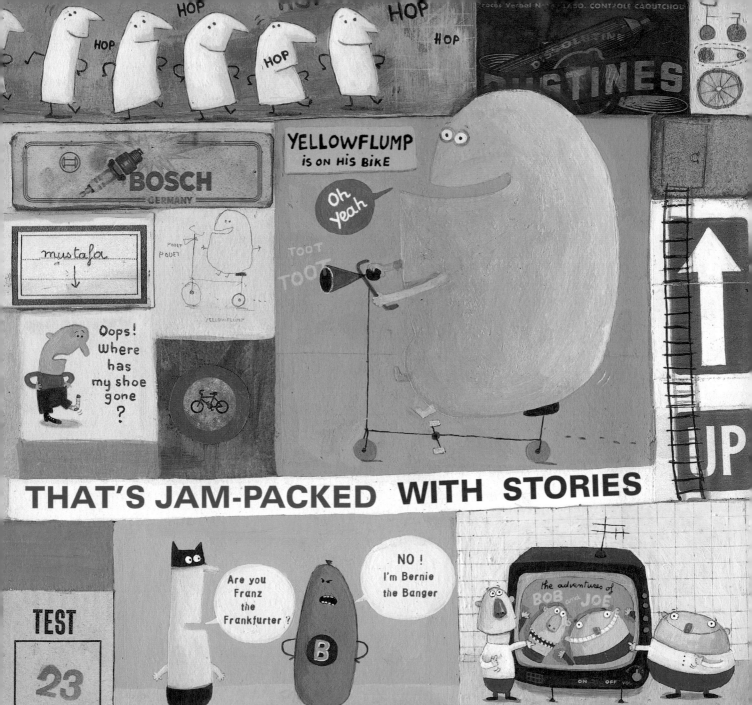

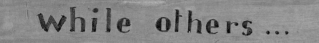

there are always
LOADS OF EXCITING THINGS HAPPENING

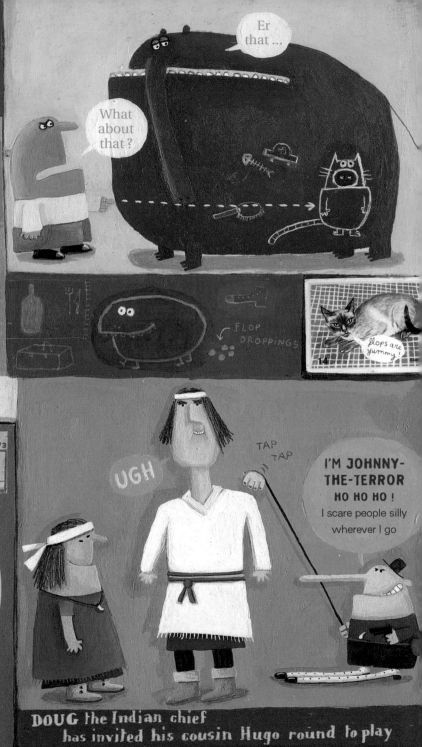

Bernie the banger, Franz the frankfurter and Colin the Chipolata have invited Inez the merguez round to watch TV

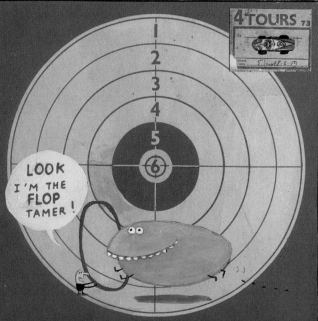

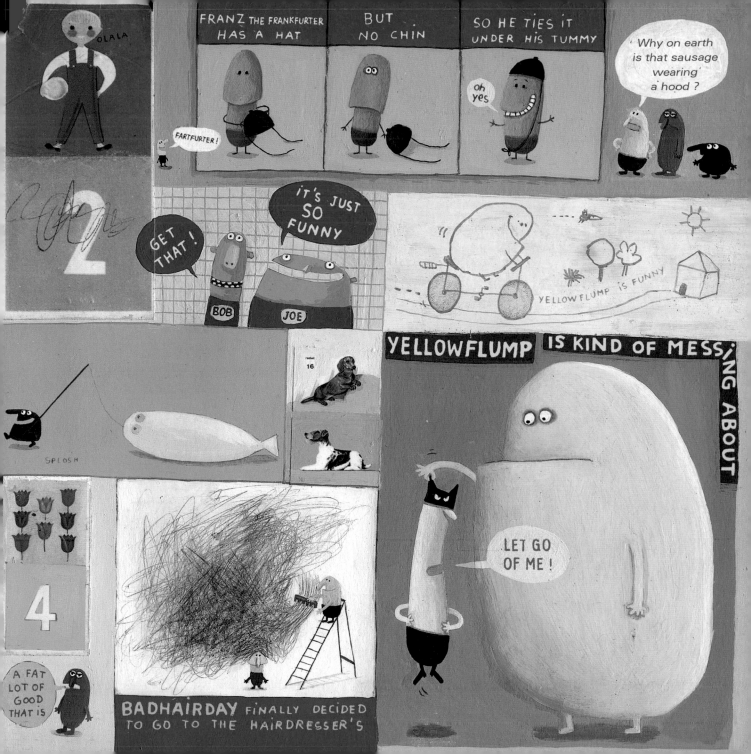

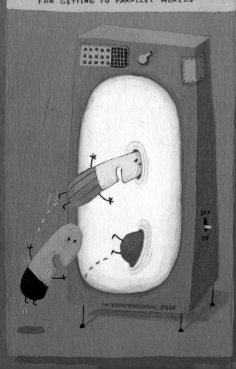

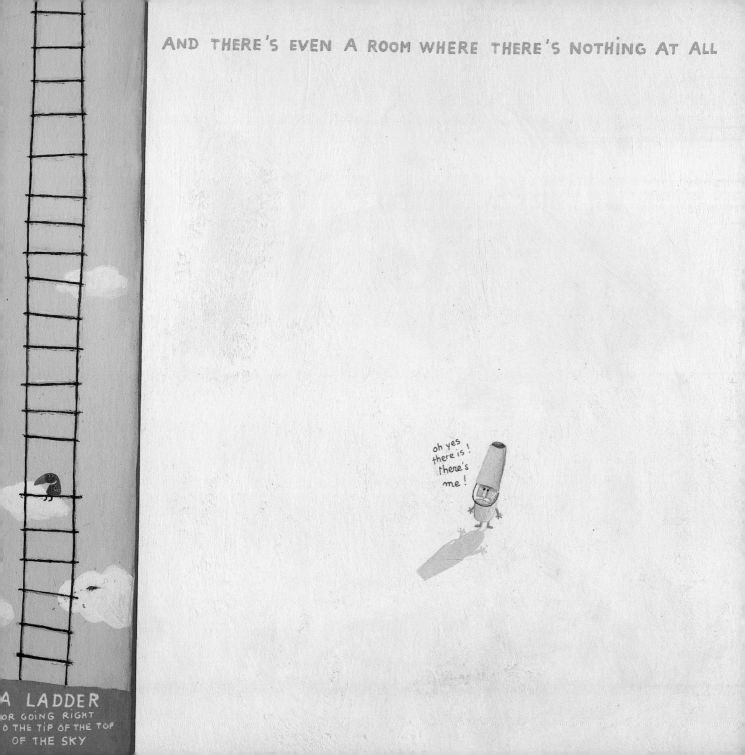

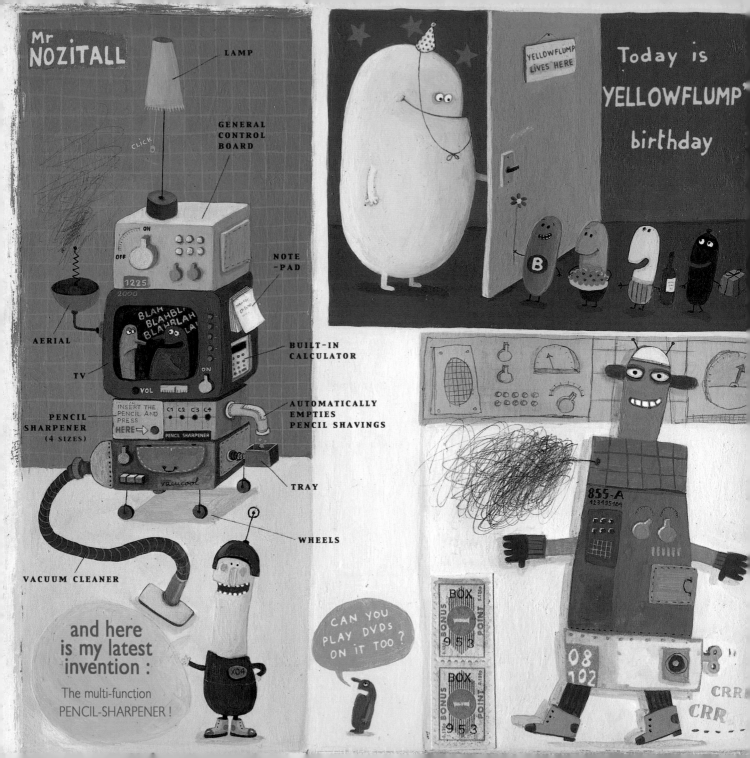

Mega-ugly AND Maxi-foul WENT BACK TO THE HAIRDRESSER'S : DRAW THEIR NEW HAIRCUTS!

How do I look ?

IT'S BETTER LIKE THIS !

here is my latest invention

Mr NOZITALL has invented a new machine : DRAW IT !

WHAT IS ALLBLU SAYING TO HIS CAT ?

MAKE UP some new FLOPS

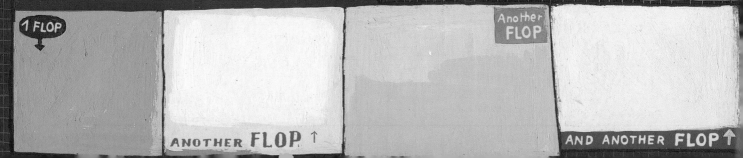

1 FLOP

Another FLOP

ANOTHER FLOP ↑

AND ANOTHER FLOP ↑

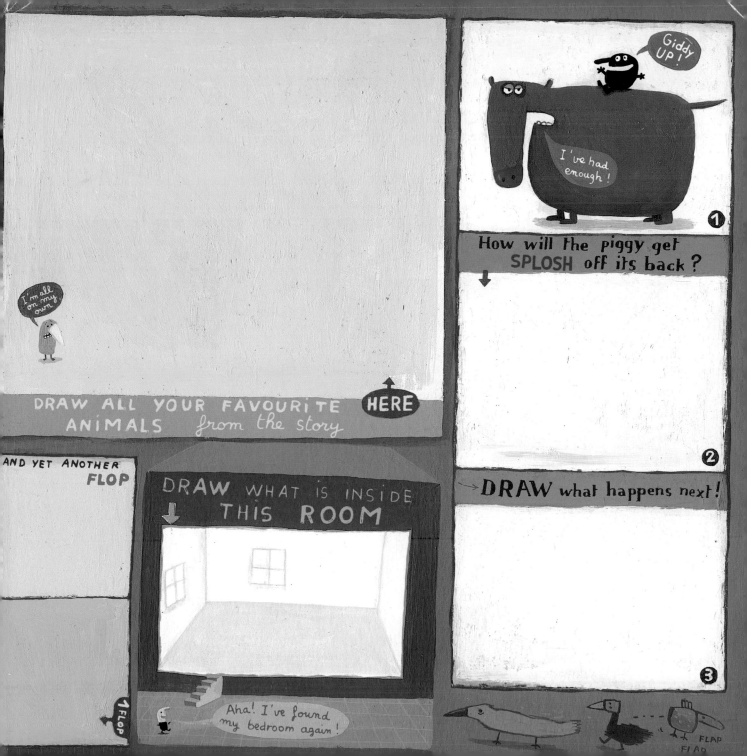